P9-AOZ-316

MODERN CURRICULUM PRESS

Robert's Robot

Alvin Granowsky
Joy Ann Tweedt
Craig L. Tweedt
Illustrated by Michael L. Denman

MODERN CURRICULUM PRESS
Cleveland • Toronto

© **1985 MODERN CURRICULUM PRESS, INC.**
13900 Prospect Road, Cleveland, Ohio 44136.

Softcover edition published simultaneously in Canada by
Globe/Modern Curriculum Press, Toronto.

Library of Congress Cataloging in Publication Data

Granowsky, Alvin, 1936-
  Robert's robot.

  Summary: After learning about robots at school, Robert falls
asleep and dreams of having a robot to do all his chores for him.
  1. Children's stories, American. (1. Robots — Fiction.
2. Dreams — Fiction)   I. Tweedt, Craig, 1950-   .
II. Tweedt, Joy, 1951-   .   III. Denman, Michael L., ill.
IV. Title.
PZ7.G76664Ro   1985   (E)   84-9083

ISBN 0-8136-5145-X (hardcover)
ISBN 0-8136-5645-1 (paperback)

1 2 3 4 5 6 7 8 9 10   86 85 84

"See this robot.
This robot can help us."

"This robot can help at work.
See it work here.

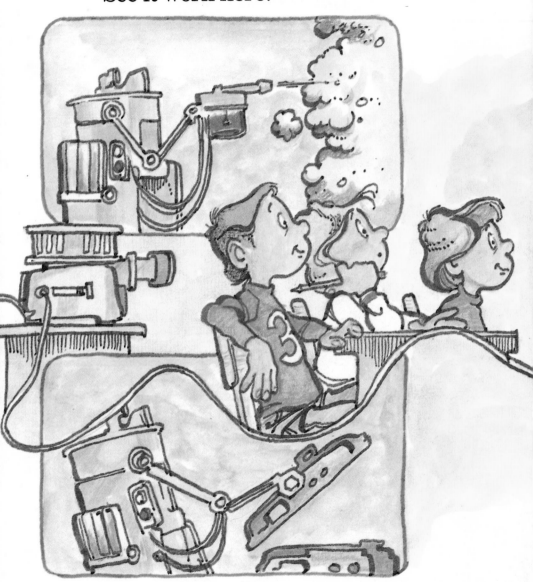

See it work there."

"A computer makes the robot work.
We tell the computer what to do.

Then the computer tells the
robot what to do."

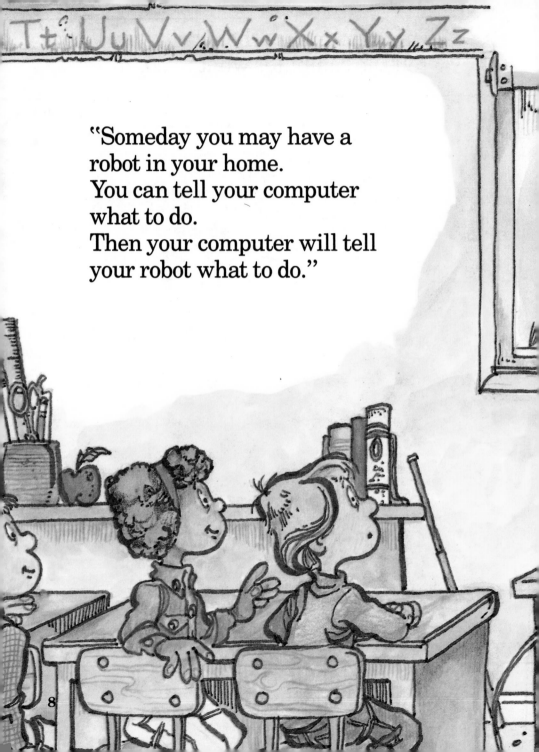

"Someday you may have a
robot in your home.
You can tell your computer
what to do.
Then your computer will tell
your robot what to do."

8

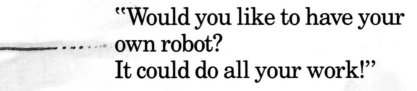

"Would you like to have your
own robot?
It could do all your work!"

9

"The robot can clean my room.
The robot can do my yard work."

"Can I have a robot?" asked Robert.
"Why do you want a robot?"
asked Mother.

"It can help me do my work,"
said Robert.
"Maybe someday you can have a robot,"
said Father.

"It's time to go to bed, Robert.
You have work to do in the morning."

It's a robot!
It's <u>my</u> robot!

16

I will make the robot work.
I will tell the computer to make
the robot work.

I will make the robot clean my room.
"Robot, clean my room."

What a clean room!
Now I will tell the robot to do my
yard work.
"Robot, do the yard work."

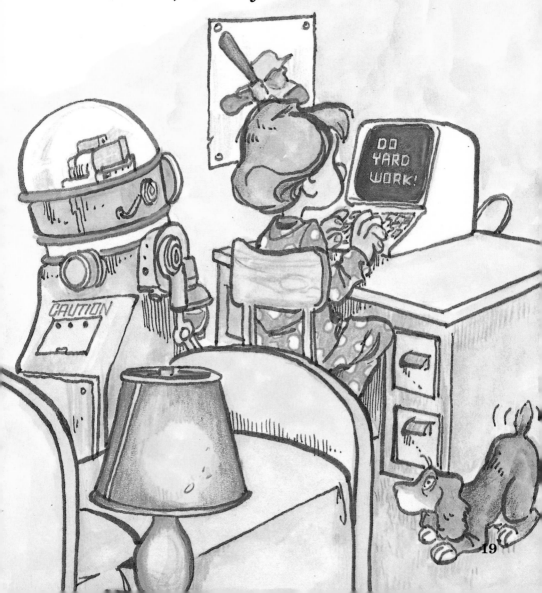

Robot is a good worker.
Now I will not have to do the
yard work.

Robot must do one more job.
"Robot, do my homework."

"Robert, get up!
You have work to do."

"All my work is done.
My robot did it," said Robert.

"Who did your work?
Robert, what are you saying?"

24

"Robot cleaned my . . .
Oh, no! Robot did not clean my
room."

25

"What about the yard?
Did robot do my yard work?"

"Oh, no! It was just a dream!
There was no robot.
It was just a dream."

"Oh, Mom, I have so much work to do!
I need a robot to help me!
I want my own robot!"

"Someday you may have one.
For now, Robert...
You will have to clean your own room.
You will have to do your yard work.
You will have to do your homework."

"So, Robert, get started.
You have a lot of work to do.
You have no robot to help you!"

"Okay, Mom, I'll do my own work for now.
Someday, I will have a robot.
You just wait and see."

ROBERT'S ROBOT

Word Count: 92
Readability: 1.7

a
about
all
and
are
asked
at

bed

can
clean(ed)
computer
could

did
do
done
dream

father
for

get
go
good

had
have
help
here
home
homework

I
I'll
in
is
it
it's

job
just

like
lot
love

.

make(s)
many
may
maybe
me
mom
more
morning
mother
much
must
my

need
no
not
now

of
oh
okay
one
own

Robert
robot
room

said
saying
see
so
someday
started

tell(s)
the
then
there
things
this
time
to

up
us

wait
want
was
we
what
who
why
will
wish
work(er)
would

yard
you
your